Hello, Family Members,

Learning to read is one of the most important accomplishments of early childhood. **Hello Reader!** books are designed to help children become skilled readers who like to read. Beginning readers learn to read by remembering frequently used words like "the," "is," and "and"; by using phonics skills to decode new words; and by interpreting picture and text clues. These books provide both the stories children enjoy and the structure they need to read fluently and independently. Here are suggestions for helping your child *before*, *during*, and *after* reading:

Before
- Look at the cover and pictures and have your child predict what the story is about.
- Read the story to your child.
- Encourage your child to chime in with familiar words and phrases.
- Echo read with your child by reading a line first and having your child read it after you do.

During
- Have your child think about a word he or she does not recognize right away. Provide hints such as "Let's see if we know the sounds" and "Have we read other words like this one?"
- Encourage your child to use phonics skills to sound out new words.
- Provide the word for your child when more assistance is needed so that he or she does not struggle and the experience of reading with you is a positive one.
- Encourage your child to have fun by reading with a lot of expression . . . like an actor!

After
- Have your child keep lists of interesting and favorite words.
- Encourage your child to read the books over and over again. Have him or her read to brothers, sisters, grandparents, and even teddy bears. Repeated readings develop confidence in young readers.
- Talk about the stories. Ask and answer questions. Share ideas about the funniest and most interesting characters and events in the stories.

I do hope that you and your child enjoy this book.

—Francie Alexander
Reading Specialist,
Scholastic's Learning Ventures

For Chris and Melissa

The author thanks Manny Campana
for his contribution to this book.

ISBN: 0-439-15433-2

Library of Congress Cataloging-in-Publication Data

Bridwell, Norman.
  The cat and the bird in the hat : story and pictures by Norman Bridwell.
   p. cm.— (Hello reader! Level 1)
  "Cartwheel Books."
  Summary: After quarrelling over ownership of a hat, Spats the cat and
Bird find that by sharing it they create a wonderful friendship.
  ISBN 0-439-15433-2 (pb)
  [1. Cats—Fiction. 2. Birds—Fiction 3. Hats—Fiction 4. Sharing—
Fiction.] I. Title. II. Series.
PZ7.B7633 Cat 2000
[E]—dc21   99-046224
12 11   08 09

Printed in the U.S.A.
March 2000

The Cat and the Bird in the Hat

story and pictures by Norman Bridwell

Hello Reader! — Level 1

SCHOLASTIC INC. Cartwheel ·B·O·O·K·S· ®

New York Toronto London Auckland Sydney
Mexico City New Delhi Hong Kong

Once there was a cat named Spats.
He was near-sighted.

He couldn't see where he was going.

One day, while taking a walk,
Spats found a hat.
It was a fine hat.
Spats put it on.

But something was
wrong with the hat.

A bird was living in the hat!

Spats asked the bird to leave.
But the bird didn't want to
leave the hat.

While they were talking about it . . .

Spats and the bird met
a little girl named Milly.

The bird took back the hat.
"It's my hat," said Spats.
"It's my hat," said the bird.

Milly said, "Why can't you *both* enjoy the hat?"

"Bird, you take the top.
Cat, you take the bottom."

And they did.
But they were not very happy.

When the bird said go right,
Spats wanted to go left.
When Spats said *no*,
the bird said *yes*.

"Look out," said the bird.
"There's a big dog right
in front of us!"

The bird led Spats to the nearest tree.

Soon the dog went away.
Spats thanked the bird for her help.

Then he climbed down the tree.

"I smell something good to eat,"
said Spats.
And his nose led them to a hot dog.
They shared it.

Then Spats took a catnap,
and the bird looked out for dogs.

All summer long they shared the hat.
They had fun swimming.

They had picnics in the park.
It was a good summer.

One day the leaves began to fall.
The bird began to put twigs and
grass in the hat.

The bird brought Spats a wool
scarf that she found.
It began to snow.
But Spats didn't mind.
His neck was warm.

The bird didn't have to fly south.
Winter was as much fun as summer.

They even made a snowcat.
What a wonderful winter it was!

One sunny morning,
the snow went away.
Spats saw a flower.

It was spring!
And in the hat
there was a new sound.

Spats ran as fast as he could
to find Milly.
He had news for her.

"Milly," he said. "You have babies . . .
I mean I have . . .
I mean *the bird* has babies!"
"Spats," said Milly. "You have a family!"

And they all lived happily ever after.